Crazy, crazy, crazzyyy

CRAZY

LIKE MY

MAMA

Crazy, crazy, crazzyyy

By **Brooke Dale**

Dedicated to :
Those who hear the voices , especially when they
Dont want to... I hear YOU !

Create Inspire Grow Publishing

Crazy, crazy, crazzyyy

Chapters

Crazy Like My Mama

He said she must be crazy like her mother and it may be true. So, what should her next move be? Is it to chase him around a two-story two-family flat with a mini sledgehammer until he hides behind a refrigerator and falls asleep too? Or do you want to listen to her recite the "Crazy, I was Crazy Once" song 50 times back to back like singing the "Wheels on the Bus go Roun' and Round" like she had to? Now that's crazy!

Why do you choose to attack her with the harshness of your words when you truly mean them about yourself? How can you say things about the one you say you love and yet retract them with excuses of anger?

FLASHBACK

It is 10:14 p.m., and we are speeding, going 74 down the highway on the open road with only the lightweight scattered highway patrol out, and he's glaring at me. What's that look? Or is that the headlights in your eye? Nigga, please. All this because you can't deal with your own inadequacies and shortcomings? Where is your discipline Gam, huh? What the fuck did you do? Why are you staring at me, and you just have nothing to say. Yea, you love going off on me cuz you think ya fly, wit ya curly hair and beard and shit. Damn, you are sexy as fuck though.

ONE YEAR EARLIER

See, that was my problem. That was me. Oh, my apologies.

Allow me to introduce myself. I'm always getting trapped up. I'm
Tracy, pleased to meet you! I seem to always be getting my shit together
and *BAM, BOOM, POW*, the bullshit! Well, back to it. I seem to be
always getting caught up in the fantasy and quick to forget about reality.
I guess that's the escape into my brain where I probably shouldn't be.
Anyway, I met Gambino, Gam for short, visiting my family back east.
Gam was fly in every sense of the word. He wasn't a talker, but he
wasn't quiet. He wasn't flashy, but he wasn't lame. He was sexy with
caramel skin, curly black hair, built up, but not like a prison nigga. I
mean everything was just right. It was something about him that had me
stuck. Even when I went back to Cali, I couldn't let this dude go. Was it
the lack of intimacy/sex in my life or that look he gave me life we were

supposed to be together from the moment we met. Whatever it was, the intensity was immense, and it never disappeared. The dude I was with at the time was dropped instantaneously, and a month later Gam came to Cali to visit his cousins. He came to see me, too and he never left.

FALLEN

That month seemed more like a year, and as quickly as the time seemed like it passed, the issues came. The jealousy began to roll like the tides. It began with simplicity and cuteness. Gam played in my phone, and we answered each other's phones. He made cute jokes like let me see who keep texting my wife— "*wife, ok*", picked my outfits, and bought all my clothes. I thought it was the life. What girl wouldn't, right?

It soon escalated to giving me curfews like a teenager, what NOT to wear, how long something needed to be, what not to eat too much of, and who not to be around. It was sweet because after all, he was my man, and he was only looking out for me, right. Somehow, though, things just didn't seem right.

I heard a voice. *"He doesn't run us. We run us."* What the hell? What was that?

Time moved but not much. Gam's jealousy would grow, and MY obsession for him grew even more. It was as if I needed him to obsess over me now. I needed him to love me more and more. I needed him to pay attention to my weight, my looks, my outfits, and me. When he didn't ask me where I was going, I got angry. When he didn't notice what I was wearing or say anything to me standing in front of him naked, we argued. I began to feel like he didn't even see me anymore. After a year, I'm old to you already, nigga.

"It's something new," the voice says. What the fuck is that? Ugh.

I called my best friend Nicci so that we can meet up because I need to talk. I just need my girl's ear right now and for her to tell me I'm not crazy because I'm really feeling like something's going on with Gam. She picks up, and I just let loose. After calming me down, we said we would meet up later this evening. I walked through the kitchen and Gam is in the family room watching the game.

I stop on the side of the couch and say, "Babe, Nicci and I are gonna go kick it later. I'm just telling you now so that you don't make plans."

He doesn't even look my way. I walked upstairs.. I'm silently crying as I'm pacing the floor for what feels like hours and hours. All of a sudden, I heard Gam's phone, and the conversation just didn't seem clear. His words were short like, mm-hmm, ok, alright. Like 30, ok. Ya know that kind of thing.

BETRAYAL

So it's about seven o'clock, and Gam is about to leave, and I am too. I start to walk out the door, and Gam asks me where I'm going.

"Excuse me! What are you talking about, I told you I was leaving to go out with Nicci," I said.

"Nawl, you chill," he said and slammed the door.

I followed him outside in the driveway and said, "Well, I'll just come with you.   "I'm straight', he said.   What? You're straight? Whatever! I mean...

"What do you mean you straight? Gam, we go everywhere together, everywhere, and now today it's a problem?" I scream at him as I'm pulling on the handle to the truck. We have been together over a year, and this nigga always has tabs on me, but now all of a sudden he doesn't want me around. Now it's not like I can't jump in my whip and bounce, but that's not the point. The point is he up to something and running around the streets won't get me the answer.

"What the fuck are you doing, Tracy?" Gam yells.

"Open the door'" I said.

"Tracy, get the fuck off my truck!" he yelled back

"Dude, I promise you. If you leave tonight, it'll be your last night, and you know I'm serious," I returned.

Gam paused, and he gave me this look that I never saw before. He walked around to the side of the truck was on, put his arms around me as if he was gonna hug me, and simultaneously said as he was throwing me to the pavement ,"BITCH, GET THE FUCK OFF MY SHIT AND TAKE YO CRAZY ASS IN THAT HOUSE!".

I sat there, frozen, as I watched the lights of his Infiniti truck speed out of our driveway. I felt like I was in a movie, a bad version of an afterschool special about domestic violence.

Still unable to move, cold and in shock, watching the rainfall and the moonlight up the quiet deserted subdivision, I could only think to myself and see the images of another day. Was it tomorrow or the next day? I could see it so clearly.The front was surrounded with EMS trucks, police cars, caution tape and red water flowing down the drains. Sirens are ringing in the air and lights are brightening the sky. Was I foreseeing his death, mine or someone else's?

I picked myself up and went inside, showered and got dressed, pampered myself prettier than I had in a very long time.

I thought maybe I was tripping and that I could make it up to my baby. I called Gam's phone to see when he would be home. I wanted to cook something special and of course be the dessert. Well, before my call went through, he called me instead by MISTAKE and to my surprise what did I hear?

"Ooh, Gam baby look at this."

Wh…What the fuck is that? No, it couldn't be. My best…my best friend's voice. That muthafuckin' BITCH!

Nicci, are you serious. This low down dirty bitch. So this is why she didn't answer.

This is why she is always agreeing with his ass.

This is why she is suddenly unavailable. She is unavailable because she is available to get dick up her ass. She's out with my man, calling him baby. I can't believe this. How could they do this to me? It sounds like they're shopping. Oh my god, oh my god.

"Kill her," says the voice. *"Tracy, you have to kill them both."*

"STOP TALKING TO ME!"

I saw red… and then black.

I remember when my mother would have a psychotic episode when I was little. She would say she saw colors and then things would change. The world would get bright and then suddenly extremely dark. We would always see the darkness in her eyes, but never the light, never the so-called brightness. Well, now I get it. I still didn't see the brightness. I only saw blood red if that counts.

THE LAPSE

The black faded to gray and for hours, I felt numb. After a while I forgot. I looked up, and Gam was lying on my lap sleeping. A bowl of shrimp penne was sitting on the table next to me with a half-smoked blunt in the ashtray alongside two glasses of half drank tequila, and a half drank bottle next to that. WTF!

The next morning consisted of sunny skies, birds chirping, pancakes, and coffee. There was minimal conversation and no mention of Gam being with Nicci, or the fight before he left. As we both prepared to leave for the evening, I noticed a receipt halfway hanging out of Gam's pants that he had on yesterday. It was from my favorite restaurant, Mitchell's Fish Market. Who? No, he did not take my best friend to my favorite place. The nerve of this nigga and this bitch! So now, I'm like Inspector Gadget. Now, I wanna go through everything. I'm furious all over again. He is crazy beyond crazy, but he is going to see crazier from me.

Low and behold what do I come across inside a jacket pocket but a folded up jewelry bag. First of all, I don't see the point of keeping evidence. If you're going to do anything suspect, get rid of the evidence. This nigga is keeping receipts and jewelry bags like the dumbest criminal. So, this is really how he is going to play me.

In my haste, I neglected one small but HUGE detail that just made my stomach drop into the soles of my feet. This other woman is my best friend. I immediately fell to my closet floor and started to cry. My heart hurt so badly because of the two people I loved to my core. I'm living a fucking cliché of a bad ghetto novel mixed with a horrible made for TV movie.

My mind is racing while he's in the shower. I wanna electrocute his ass, and all I keep seeing is red and hearing these fucking voices.

Then all I heard is *"Don't trust him."*

"Shut up!"

"What you talking about now, damn!" Gam yells from the shower.

"I'm not talking to you!" I yelled back.

"Crazy bitch," Gam mumbles.

"He's leaving you for her ya know," the voice whispered back.

I ran downstairs repeating to myself, "I'm not crazy like my mother, I'm not crazy like my mother I'm not crazy like my mother," over and over and over again. I heard the shower go off and that must've snapped me back. I looked down, and I had a butcher knife in one hand, and Gam's picture in the other. I went back to getting dressed, and we left separately.

* * *

The day was really long. Gam went about his day. I called Nicci for a nice girl's day out. My phone rang and it was Gam. He wanted to meet at the Casino to have drinks and just chill for a while. It's always a tossup because Gam and gambling don't always mix. I mean the man's name is "Gam" for a reason. He once won 247K in 24one night, binged the week, balled out, and lost 180K back, didn't blink an eye, and would tell you "that's gambling, baby". He also hit licks so hard that we have lived beautifully, and he's lost so badly that I thought we would never recover all in the little year or so since I've been with him, so I can only imagine his life before me. Needless to say, when Gam wants to "go have a drink at the "Ino" and chill, I never know what the night may end up like. However, this particular night, I had a feeling I may be getting a little more entertainment.

MAKE UP

We hit up a couple of spots, we played a couple of slots, and by now, I was feeling good and looking good. I was actually looking to feel better. Gam stops at his homie PJ's spot for some "limelight", and we continued with the party. Now, for those who may need a quick overview let's bring you up to speed. Known in Cali as "Limelight" is done out of the "limelight, it is also known to the society as candy, sugar, blo, "the party", etc., get a fucking book, well, another book, I'm not your drug mentor.

Now I don't know about you, but in California and even back East in Philly, I have seen a lot of people party, but Gam goes too hard too fast. And let's just say I go slow and steady and made sure I got a little something extra from PJ to make sure Gam had more than enough to be satisfied. See, Gam likes to run his mouth, and this is why this is going to be a great way to see what he may slip up and say about Nicci, the jewelry bag, and everything. Nicci didn't have too much to say so, let's get back to Gam. I hit a few bumps, gave Gam a few hefty ones, and I went to hit a few more and look up, and he has the coldest look ever like he's plotting or something.

"He's gonna do something."

There's that voice. I must've zoned out hard or something. There was that voice again. What did mama do when she heard them or did she hear them at all? All of a sudden, Gam just starts screaming and yelling and cursing. He's talking to me like he never has. He's saying things like all he ever did was love me, and why am I so crazy. He watches me talk to myself.

"I never talk to myself," I told him. "You are the crazy one"

He had to be talking to me or something or maybe saw me talking to myself. What was I doing? Was I really crazy? What did I do? Or was he? He was the one cheating. He was the one on all the drugs. He was the abusive one. We argued all the way home. We were both so angry that it made me feel better about what I already knew awaited us. I just don't know if the truth may drive me truly crazy in the end.

PEACE

That day with Nicci was a good day. She got sleepy, really sleepy, and she ended up taking a nap, a long nap, in "her baby" Gam's trunk. Remember that butcher knife, well, let's just say we got a little more acquainted and I left it for Gam as a little gift in his closet in his safe. You see, he was so angry and coked up on the way home that I guess my "crazy" made him get a little rough with me. By the time we pulled up home, it was the same scene as in my mind before. There it was, caution tape, police lights, sirens, EMS trucks, and a bloodstained driveway. While we were gone, it rained. I guess my wrapping skills needed work. OOPS. Poor little Nicci's body leaked a little onto the driveway, and old lady Langston who walks her dog religiously six times a day just happened to notice the discolored rainwater and made a concerned citizen's call. The takeout receipt in her handbag, two takeout cups in the truck, the wedding ring, the knife from our kitchen hidden in his

21

closet, his truck, there lies the "mistress/ another woman", my friend, and his lies are no more.

They took Gam that night, and I remember looking into his eyes. For the first time, I saw that light before the darkness my mother spoke of. Instead of myself, I saw it in Gam.

I watched it leave from his eyes and become dark, and a part of me cried, and the other smiled just a little. I remember back when he asked am I crazy like my mother, and I wonder if I can answer honestly.

THE ANSWER

Now had I learned earlier that the jewelry bag was empty because it originally contained a box with a five-carat princess cut platinum ring,things may have gone differently. Gam intended to propose to me. Nicci, my best friend, went along because who knows your taste better than your bestie, The secrets and the lies were none other than little

22

white lies to go along with a surprise, and my favorite restaurant was merely a thank you for her and takeout for us.

So, do I feel bad you ask for setting my man up and killing my best friend? Was it extreme? Was I inside my own head and did what the voice said? I mean after all, it did say he was going to leave me for her and repeatedly called me crazy like my mother. Well, I guess the answer is no, maybe I'm just a GANGSTA LIKE MY FATHER!

......, well it looked it he was cheating

Crazy, crazy, crazzyyy

……., Tracey , talk to me …..

…. You'll be back!!